Not Fantasy

AMY LAURENS

OTHER WORKS

SANCTUARY SERIES

Where Shadows Rise
Through Roads Between
When Worlds Collide

KADITEOS SERIES

How Not To Acquire A Castle
Define Good
How Not To Ring The Hero's Bell

STORM FOXES SERIES

A Fox of Storms and Starlight

SHORTER WORKS

Darkness and Good
Dreaming Of Forests
Of Sea Foam and Blood
Trust Issues

NON-FICTION

How To Write Dogs
How To Theme
How To Create Cultures
How To Create Life
How To Map
The 32 Worst Mistakes People Make About Dogs

Find other works by the author at
www.amylaurens.com

NOT FANTASY

INKLET #33

AMY LAURENS

Inkprint PRESS

www.inkprintpress.com

Print ISBN: 978-1-925825-40-4
eBook ISBN: 9781393910794

www.inkprintpress.com

National Library of Australia Cataloguing-in-Publication Data
Laurens, Amy 1985 –
Not Fantasy
64 p.
ISBN: 978-1-925825-40-4
Inkprint Press, Canberra, Australia
1. Young Adult Fiction—Fantasy—Contemporary 2.
Young Adult Fiction—School & Education—College &
University 3. Young Adult Fiction—Short Stories

First Print Edition: May 2020
Cover image © Lilawind via Pixabay
Cover design © Inkprint Press
Interior art © Amy Laurens

NOT FANTASY

Beth stared at the blank search engine on her computer screen. "How am I going to find something for this stupid assignment that I actually *like*?"

"Oo, oo!" A bright pink pen rattled in its stand at the back of the desk. "I know, I know!"

Beth glared at it. "I don't *want* your ideas. I'm supposed to take in a *sensible* story."

Technically pens couldn't pout, but this one—Beth jokingly called it her

Muse, after its propensity for coming up with wildly implausible ideas—certainly implied it.

"Well," said the pink tortoise that sat next to the keyboard. "He said to find a story that connects with something you know, yes?"

Beth nodded.

"So what about all those magazines you read online? Surely something in one of those connects to you somehow."

"Of course, that's why I love them. But I'm pretty sure it's supposed to be a realist story." Beth wrinkled her nose.

"But the stories you read are real," said the pen.

"For a given value of real," said Beth. "Most people don't believe your world exists. People like Mr Sedriane. *Especially* Mr Sedriane." She pulled a face. "Him and his stupid prejudice against anything exciting. Gar!" She flung herself back in her chair. "I hate English!"

"There, there," said Pembe. "We'll think of something. When is it due?"

"I have to take a story to class to-morrow."

Silence filled the bedroom as they thought.

Beth exhaled and flopped face-first on the keyboard. "It's nearly ten o' clock," she mumbled. "I just want to go to bed."

Pembe snuggled into her hair. "Just find something, anything. It doesn't matter if you don't really like it. As you said, you're not getting marked on it, you just have to hand something in."

Beth turned towards Pembe and stretched her lips into a half smile. "You know what? You're right. I'm not getting marked on it. So what the hell, I'll take in one I really like."

Pembe jerked her head in concern. "Won't you get in trouble?"

"Of course not. What's he going to do, give me detention because I brought in the wrong story? Hardly." Beth righted herself and rested her fingers on the keys, ignoring the nerves in her stomach that knew Mr Sedriane might do exactly that.

⎯⎯⎯

Beth crossed her legs under the classroom desk and glanced around the room. In theory she was reading the stories everyone else had brought to class, but really, she was too nervous to concentrate.

The others never seemed to have trouble adhering to Mr Sedriane's rigid rule of 'no fantasy', but for some reason, no matter how hard she tried, she couldn't make herself like the stories without magic—and she just couldn't bring herself to choose a story for class that she didn't really like.

And it was only week two. This was going to be a long term. Stupid short story unit with its stupid teacher and his stupid rules. She should have listened to her mother and stayed in normal English, instead of trying for extension.

"Psst." The dark-haired boy sitting next to her—Paul, she thought—leaned towards her.

She glanced over and saw her story at the top of his pile.

"Cool story," he said.

"Whatever." Beth shrugged. She wasn't in the mood for barely-concealed flirting today.

"No, seriously," he said. "It's really good. It's really… you."

Beth stared at him. Maybe he was serious after all. "Thanks." She screwed up her nose. "Don't think he'll appreciate it though." She jerked her head towards the hunched figure behind the desk at the front of the room.

Paul twitched his eyebrows. "Yeah. Probably not." He shrugged. "Oh well, it's a cool story. And it's about time someone stood up to him."

Beth grinned weakly and turned away. Stood up to him? She hadn't meant the piece to be controversial, not really. But if Paul thought that, then there was little doubt that Mr Sedriane would too.

"All right class!" Up the front, Mr Sedriane clapped his hands. "Reading time is up. We'll go around the room and each of you will tell us why your story connects to you, beginning with Hannah."

Great, thought Beth. That meant she was second to last.

Some of the other stories weren't too bad, but Beth couldn't bring herself to comment. She was going to be flayed, she just knew it, and a thousand grasshoppers seemed to have taken up residence in her stomach.

"Okay, Beth."

Beth glanced up at the teacher. Tension showed around his eyes, though possibly not quite as much as she'd expected.

The class fidgeted.

"Well?" said Mr Sedriane, drumming his fingers against the desk. "Are you going to speak?"

Beth wet her lips. "I, um, chose this story because it connects to me. It's about a girl who—"

Mr Sedriane waved his hand dismissively. "Irrelevant," he pronounced. "This story is about magic, magic is not real, and this is not in any way connected to your life." He raised an eyebrow. "Unless you have the ability to speak to trees, as the main character in this story?"

Beth lowered her gaze.

"I thought not. Right. Sally?"

Out of the corner of her eye Beth saw Jess, the blonde girl with the bright green glasses who sat right up the front and had an opinion on everything, wave her hand in the air. "Excuse me, Mr Sedriane?" Jess said.

The teacher gave her his best 'you have interrupted me' look, but nodded.

"I was just wondering, I mean I, um, well…"

Beth's stomach clenched. Why was Jess so nervous?

Jess took a deep breath. "What I'm trying to say is that I don't understand why Beth can't connect to this story. The main character is still human, and still experiences human emotions."

Beth looked back at her teacher. He glowered at the students and silence smothered the room.

Beth shrank down in her seat.

"Elizabeth Scott."

She sank even lower.

"If I've told you once, I've told you a thousand times. We are in this class to learn about serious literature, not fairy stories for children."

It probably *was* nearing the thousandth time, but that didn't make it any more pleasant. Beth squirmed as her classmates stared at her.

"Class."

Their gazes snapped front-ward.

"You will all learn from this. Yes, the main character has human-like aspects. But I stress to you: *that is not that point*. This is a *literary class*. I don't care how beautiful the prose is or how fascinating the story, if you insist on bringing fairytales into this class as though we were all six-year-olds, you *will* fail. Literature, students. We are here to study literature. It is, after all, an extension class."

Beth gnawed on the inside of one cheek. "It *is* real," she muttered.

"What was that?" The professor glared at her.

'Nothing,' she meant to say, 'it was

nothing.' Instead, she leapt to her feet. Part of her was horrified and begged her to sit down and shut up, but she burst out, "It *is* real!"

A few of her classmates sniggered.

The professor rose. Under his chilling glare the class grew silent.

Beth stared back at him, hands trembling. *What have I done?* she thought. *Idiot!*

Her classmates began to fidget, but Beth refused to lower her gaze. "It is real," she said at last, quietly, calmly.

In equally calm tones, Sedriane replied. "You will see me in my office after class. For now, you may leave my classroom."

<hr>

Beth swallowed and knocked on the door.

"Come!"

She bumped the door open and licked her lips. "I'm here, sir."

He sat with his back to the door, intent on his computer screen. He waved a hand at some low, padded chairs against the wall to his right. "Sit."

Beth sat, dropping her bag at her feet. She glanced around. Unsurprisingly, the room was bare, a stark, unrelieved white. A metal frame jutted out from the wall above his desk holding a few tattered books, the window gave a murky view of the main courtyard, and the whole thing smelled vaguely of cheese.

Mr Sedriane hammered away at his keyboard and Beth tried to pretend she was there for a happier reason. But the silver birches outside glowed eerily in the fading light, and she shivered.

"Right," he said at last. Beth jumped. "You know what you are here for."

"Yes, sir," said Beth in a small voice. She hunched down in her seat and stared out the window.

"You are here, young lady, because you are one of the most disruptive, insolent students I have ever had the misfortune to teach."

Beth clenched her jaw and blinked rapidly. *I will not cry. I will not cry. My, how lovely the birches look…*

"Unfortunately," said Mr Sedriane with a sigh, "that alone is not sufficient basis for the school to allow me to fail you."

Fail? Beth bit back a gasp. She *couldn't* fail. She *never* failed. Never, ever, in her entire life! "I… I'm sorry," she murmured, risking a quick glance towards him.

He pursed his lips and considered her. "Perhaps you are, and perhaps you aren't. Next week's submission will show." He leaned closer. "Won't it."

It wasn't a question, and she nodded, trembling. "Y… Yes, sir."

"And there will be no more of this *fantasy*"—his face distorted around the word like it was a lemon—"in my class. Will there?"

Beth shook her head.

"Thank you," said Mr Sedriane. "Then, if that is all, you may go." He turned back to his computer screen.

Beth opened her mouth to say 'Thank you', and froze.

Mr Sedriane's gaze flicked over her. "Did you wish to say something?"

No! she screamed. *No! Nothing! I'm leaving, going! Now, do you hear?* But some wild impulse again took hold of her tongue, and she found herself saying, "Sir, it really is real."

His nostrils flared and the wall behind his head seemed to darken. "No," he said calmly. "It isn't."

Something about the darkness around his head captured her attention and, focused on it, Beth stood. "Yes. It is."

The darkness flared as though the wall was cracking.

"No!" He jumped to his feet. "No, it *isn't!*"

Beth stepped closer, drawn by the darkness that crackled its way across the wall. She reached out a hand to it.

"NO!"

Beth jumped as Mr Sedriane splash-ed a glass of blue liquid at the wall then grabbed her by the wrist. She yelped as he threw her back against the chairs, then stared up at him, pulse racing. What had she done?

He leaned over her. She shrank back until there was nowhere left to shrink, and still he came closer, closer, until his nose nearly touched her own.

"Miss Scott, you listen to me, and you listen to me well. *Fantasyland does not exist.*"

A light flashed outside the window and Beth shrieked.

Mr Sedriane glanced outside. "It's just a security light," he said tightly. "Are you listening to me?"

Beth nodded.

"Repeat after me: There is no such thing as Fantasyland. There is… Go on, say it." He narrowed his eyes and nodded at her.

"There…" She swallowed as another light flashed outside the window. "There is no such thing…" The light outside the window grew brighter and Beth tore her gaze away from her teacher. "…as Fantasy…" She gasped. "Land!"

Beth leaped to her feet, knocking Mr Sedriane aside. Surely—*surely*—that had not been a *unicorn* she'd just seen at the window!

She cried out as the professor's bony fingers gripped her shoulder and steered her towards the door. "Get. Out. Now."

She snatched up her bag as he shoved her out of the office. He slammed the door, leaving Beth staring immobile at the opposite wall.

The teacher next door poked her head out into the corridor. "Everything okay?"

"Er..." Beth gave herself a little shake. "Um, yeah. Yeah, everything's fine." She shouldered her backpack and smiled at the woman. "Thanks." *I am so going to have to drill Pembe about this.*

"And then," said Beth, leaning in close to the tortoise and pen perched on the edge of her desk, "you'll never guess what I saw."

"What? What?" The pen bobbed, almost knocking its plastic stand over.

Pembe rolled her eyes. "Settle, will you?"

Beth grinned. "Oh, I think this warrants some excitement. It was a unicorn!"

Pembe stared at her in astonishment. "A real, live unicorn?"

"Uh huh." Beth's grin broadened. "A real, live unicorn."

The pen rattled around its stand. "But that's unheard of! Stop teasing us!"

Beth straightened. "I'm not teasing you. It's the truth. What do you think it means?" she asked Pembe.

The tortoise rubbed her head against her shell, thinking. "Well," she said at last. "The borders must have been very thin there this evening for some reason. Unicorns have by far the most trouble crossing the borders; they must have been very weak indeed for you to have seen it right there outside the window.

Beth nodded. "That's what I thought. Do you think the cracks have anything to do with it?"

Pembe waggled her head. "I've never heard of cracks of darkness appearing along the borders before, but stranger things have happened. It's all very puzzling," she finished after a moment.

"I know." Beth sighed and folded her arms on the desk. "I can't help but feel I'm missing something very important here."

They fell silent, the tick of the clock keeping time to their thoughts. *What am I missing?* thought Beth. *Something's not right in all of this.*

"That's it!" The pen's shrill voice broke through the silence. Beth and Pembe jumped.

"What," said Beth. "What is it?"

"And must you give us all heart attacks like that?" grumbled Pembe. "You do realise that you can't share your news with us if we're dead?"

The pen stuck its feathers up at Pembe. "You're just jealous 'cause I've figured it out and you haven't," it said.

"Leave it," said Beth with a warning glare at Pembe. "Now, what's your idea?" she asked the pen.

"It's Fantasyland," it said, spinning in a circle.

"Pen, a cockroach could have told us that much!" Pembe glared at it menacingly.

"Pembe!"

"Sorry!"

The pen stuck its feathers up again.

"Pen…" said Beth.

"Okay, okay. So, it's Fantasyland. We all know that." It jerked rudely at Pembe. "But the question is *why*?"

"Yes," interrupted Pembe. "*Thank you*—"

"And," the pen continued loudly, "I think I know the answer. What did you say the professor asked you to repeat?"

"There is no such thing as Fantasyland," said Beth.

"Yes!" The pen skittered around again. "That's it! It's Fantasyland!"

Pembe shambled towards the pen. "Pen, I swear, if you don't stop speaking cryptically…"

The pen straightened. "Isn't it obvious? The name of the thing attracts the thing. Basic principle of magic. In asking you to name it, he brought it closer!"

Beth nodded. "Actually, that makes sense. Well done, Penny."

The pen stuck its feathers up at Pembe again.

"Yes, yes, all right," said Pembe grudgingly as she halted. "Well done."

"So," said Beth, leaning back in her chair. "By naming it he brought it closer. But…" She paused as a thought struck her. "It doesn't come closer when we name it. Why only for him?"

Pembe's eyes lit up. "What does he look like, again?"

Beth wrinkled her brow. "Um, just taller than me, dark hair, fair skin, skinny little nose, weak chin…"

"Ears?" said Pembe.

Beth took in a sharp breath as she realised where Pembe was heading.

"Not sure, but it would fit, wouldn't it? If he's an elf…" She screwed up her nose. "But why is he so averse to fantasy, then? Wouldn't being an elf make him like it more?"

Pembe gave her a wicked grin. "Not if he's one of the Banished. That might explain the dark cracks, too; 'The Darkness lurks behind those who fall', remember?"

Beth grinned back. "I love that line." She adored the whole poem, it was the piece that had made her fall in love with fantasy to begin with, but that line in particular always gave her shivers.

The pen rattled. "So," it said. "Now that we've established I'm a genius, not to put a damper on things or anything, but… What are you going to do?"

Beth bit her lip, thinking. Then she laughed.

"What, what?" said the pen.

Beth caught Pembe's eye. "What do you think?"

"What?" said the pen.

"Yes. Oh yes." Pembe grinned up at her.

"What?"

Beth pressed a finger down on top of the pen, halting its skittery jumps. "We test our theory."

"And how do we do that?"

Beth raised her eyebrows. "I believe," she said, grin dimpling her cheeks, "I have a story to write."

⟵——— ▪

Beth pressed her forehead against the cool wall. *Go on,* she thought. *Just open the door, and take a seat.*

She shivered as somewhere another door opened, sending a blast of cold air down the corridor. *At least it'll be warm in there…* She snorted. Warm as hell, probably. She'd seen the challenge in Sedriane's eyes when she'd handed in her story this morning; he must have known what she'd done even then.

So. She couldn't chicken out now. If she did, he'd win, and she'd never get to find out if their conclusions about the cracks of darkness were right.

Beth squared her shoulders, took a deep breath, and opened the door. The other students already had their pile of papers for the day, and on the one spare desk sat another pile. For her. He'd known she would come.

Avoiding eye contact, Beth slunk in and sat. Half-heartedly, she began to shuffle through the papers. A title caught her eye, and she pulled the page out. *Where Shadows Rise*, it read. Beth frowned. Someone else had written fantasy?

She flicked through the pages again. *Lady Of The Lake*. That sounded like fantasy, too. Beth skimmed the page, pulse racing. It was, it was fantasy, magic and amulets and quests and all.

She snuck a glance at the professor. He caught her eye. Beth felt a rush of adrenalin.

Livid. He was absolutely livid.

Holding her gaze, the professor stood and padded over to her desk. "Elizabeth," he said softly. "Please stand up."

The general rustling of paper ceased, and Beth felt eyes boring into her. She stood.

"I hope you have seen, this week, how your lies have encouraged others to make their own?"

And that's such *a bad thing,* she thought, but kept silent.

"You admit, then, that they are lies?" Sedriane's voice was still low, but an edge of menace had crept into it and his glare seemed to drill right into her mind.

It would be so much easier to lie, she thought. *To just agree with him, and make it all go away.*

She bit the inside of her lip, torn.

Her bag twitched, bumping gently against her leg.

Yes, she thought. *You're right. I have to tell the truth.* She took a deep breath. "I thought it might come to this." Around her, students gasped. Beth ignored them, reaching into her bag.

"Miss Scott, you are impertinent to the extreme. This is neither the time not the place—"

Beth placed Pembe gently onto her desk and stared at the professor. The students gasped again.

"Is it real?" someone murmured.

Beth turned to face the class. "Yes," she said. "Yes, she is real."

Pembe tromped across the desk and one or two of the girls squealed. Beth bit back a giggle. *This is no time to get hysterical,* she told herself sternly, and turned back to the professor.

To her surprise, Professor Sedriane stood rooted in place, leaning back from Beth's desk with a twisted expression of disgust. "Get that… *thing* out of my classroom immediately."

Beth smiled. "No," she said, voice even and polite. "Not until you admit that I wasn't lying."

The professor tore his gaze away from Pembe and glared at Beth. "Never. You were lying, you are. This is some kind of trick!"

Beth raised an eyebrow. "Fantasyland," she said firmly. It was just one word, but it shook the room.

Black cracks began to form across the front wall, the whiteboard looking like it had been festooned by cobwebs.

The professor glanced over his shoulder at them, licking his lips nervously. "No," he said. "No, you can't."

Beth picked Pembe up off the desk and stepped towards him. "Yes," she said. "I can."

The professor edged away from her, closer to the cracks.

"It *is* real, isn't it, Professor." She held Pembe up in his face.

Blood drained from his face, leaving him even whiter than usual. "No," he said. "I won't go back! You can't make me!"

The cracks widened.

"Actually," said Beth, "you're right. I can't. But that," she nodded at the darkness, "can."

"No!" He clutched at his desk, hunching over on it, clinging to it like it could save his life. "No, you can't take me back! I didn't do it! It wasn't me!"

"The cracks say otherwise," said Beth. "You know perfectly well they wouldn't come for you if you'd been *wrongly* banished."

Sedriane's eyes lit up in anger. "What would you know, you filthy little *human*?"

Beth fought back a wave of her own anger. *Calm,* she thought. *Just stay calm, and the cracks will do their job.* She looked down at him, spread out on the top of his desk, alternately whimpering as he watched the cracks creep closer and gnashing his teeth at Pembe.

And Beth felt her anger dissipate for real. "You know what?" she said, voice strangely flat. "I think I actually feel sorry for you."

The Professor's face contorted. "No," he snarled. "No, you *don't.*"

Beth shrugged. "Whatever. Either way, I think it's time to say goodbye. *Fantasyland,*" she finished emphatically. In response, the cracks of darkness yawned wider.

Sedriane opened his mouth to reply, but his eyes went wide and he froze.

The darkness crept up his legs, pinning him, erasing him, creeping, creeping, until it reached his neck, his ears, his nose…And he was gone.

There was a low rumble, and the darkness disappeared.

Beth hung her head, hugging Pembe to her chest.

"Well done," whispered Pembe.

Beth smiled wryly. "Yeah." She turned back to the class, who sat staring at her, more than half with their chins hanging slack. "Er, class dismissed?"

At the sound of her voice, Paul gave himself a shake. He blinked at her, then began to clap.

The other students broke out of their stupor and joined in, clapping and cheering and pumping the air with their fists.

Beth broke into a grin. "Thanks."

<hr>

Beth stood outside the classroom door the next day, wondering what awaited her.

"So."

She turned as Paul sidled up to her, silly grin on his face. "So," she said.

"Nice work yesterday."

"Thanks."

He shoved his hands into his pockets. "You, er… You wanna get a coffee later?"

Beth's heart skipped a beat. "Um. Okay?" *Argh!* She screeched at herself. *He so only likes you 'cause you're the new hero! Say no, say no!*

But it was too late, and he was grinning like a madman, and she didn't have the heart to change her answer.

Besides. He was kind of cute.

Jess of the green glasses walked up. "Hey."

Beth smiled. "Hey."

"So, who do you think they'll have to replace old Sedderpants?" she said.

Paul shrugged. "Dunno, but I think we're about to find out." He nodded to the door, which creaked open. "Shall we?" He gestured and Beth, smiling shyly, ducked through the door in front of him.

And froze. "Oh, no."

Paul bumped into her. "What?" he said. "What is it?"

Beth stepped aside to allow the rest of the class to filter in. One by one they entered until the entire class stood plastering the back wall, mouths forming perfect 'o's.

In front of them, behind the teacher's desk, sat a tall, red-skinned creature. Its woolly legs ended in hooves that rested on the desk, and its tail swished lazily underneath.

"Ah," said the demon, getting to his feet. "You must be my new class. The one who loves fantasy so much."

A few students nodded vaguely.

The creature grinned, showing pearly white fangs. "Excellent."

He rose from the desk and stalked towards them. "You wanted fantasy," he said. "You got it."

THE MAKING OF
NOT FANTASY

Secret confession: this is a revenge story. The only one I've ever written, actually, and honestly it's not revenge so much as it is catharsis.

Because, yes, I did have a professor who was puzzled to the extreme about why so many of his students wanted to write fantasy stories—though he was a reasonably nice human being and, rather than banning us from doing so, recommended we read Ursula Le Guin's marvellous book on writing fantasy.

Still. It was fun to revisit that time in this story, and although the sting has diminished with time, I suspect I wasn't quite so chill about this all when I actually *wrote* this story.

I do remember it was part of the mostly-weekly short story challenge I was doing with friends on Critique Circle, back in circa 2007 or 2008 when I—and some friends—were trying to learn to write *short*.

That's not *particularly* relevant; what is relevant is that this story was the result of some advice given by another of my friends in that group: write a story for catharsis, a story to remind you that whatever kind of stories you want to tell, they are worth telling. That your stories are yours because they are you, which means staying true to what you want to say and what you want to write.

Write a story that proves that, to yourself if to no one else.

And so I did, and it was cathartic—even if I do feel a tiny bit mean ;)

DOWNLOAD YOUR FREE EBOOK

When you buy a print book from Inkprint Press, we like to say THANK YOU by offering you the ebook for free!

Please head to www.inkprintpress.com/inklets/33/ and the use the coupon 33INKLET to get your copy of this Inklet in epub AND mobi today!
(Coupon will only work once.)

Read more by Amy Laurens!

WHERE SHADOWS RISE

CHAPTER ONE

THE DOORBELL RANG. That doesn't sound exciting in and of itself, but let me assure you: it was the most heart-pounding thing to happen all week. It was my birthday, I was home alone, and because of the stupid witness protection business, I'd been stuck in the house all summer. I hadn't even been allowed out to see friends, because we'd arrived in town at the end of last year with only three school weeks to go—so I didn't have any friends.

Well. I had friends, but they were back in Melbourne, and I wasn't allowed to contact them for fear someone would track down our new location. Lucky me.

Anyway, it was my birthday, I was alone because Mum and Dad had gone to do something regarding birthday surprises and Anna had inexplicably chosen to go with them, and the doorbell had just rung. I stared at the closed door, heart pounding, while our chocolate Labrador, Veve, tried to chew it down. Was I going to open it?

Of course I was going to open it. The chances of it being a mobster were slim to none; for starters, a mobster wouldn't have rung the bell.

I opened it.

"Miss Tanning?" The deliveryman raised a questioning eyebrow and cocked a digital pen at me.

I nodded, heart flip-flopping, and scrawled a fair impersonation of my signature on the digital pad.

He handed over a small, brown-paper parcel with a handwritten address, and departed.

I closed the door behind him, throat dry, and stared down at Veve. On the one hand, yay birthday present. On the other, holy crap, someone had our address. That was *not* a good thing.

It became even less of a good thing when I noticed that the parcel was indeed addressed to a Miss Tanning: a Miss *Anna* Tanning, as in my sister, not me, Emma Tanning.

Anger bubbled up in my chest, hot and tight, and the parcel protested in my grip.

Veve whined softly.

"How could she *do* this?" I whispered to Veve.

I turned the parcel over. It was from Kade, Anna's frogging ex-boyfriend. Who apparently wasn't an 'ex' after all.

Urgh. I ground my teeth. "You know what?" I asked Veve.

She looked up at me with her liquid brown eyes, tongue lolling as she smiled.

"Screw it. If Anna can get interstate mail from people who aren't even supposed to know we exist anymore, you and I can go for a walk on my birthday. What do you think?"

They say dogs don't speak English, but Veve sure as heck knew the word 'walk'—though I think in her vocabulary it was something closer to 'Magical Trip To Disneyland' and less like 'Comparatively Bland Meander Through Trees'.

She tucked her tail right under her butt and shot down the hall, whirling in frantic circles a few times at the end before pelting back as I retrieved her lead from the drawer in the front cabinet.

I rolled my eyes as I clipped her lead onto her collar. For my troubles, I got slimed right up the nostrils. "You're disgusting, you know that?" I wiped off the worst of the dog slobber on the shoulder of my shirt. She just grinned.

Out on the street, she leapt and twisted madly. "Hair-brain," I told her, snapping the lead to get her attention. "It's just a walk."

She just snorted—and stiffened. I followed her gaze to where a flock of corellas pecked their way through the dry grass at the end of the street.

"Veve!"

My shout was in vain: the lead burned through my fingers and Veve shot down the road, a chocolate bullet howling death and destruction for all things feathered.

I cursed her to the lower circles of doggie hell. Which probably involved, I don't know, a world devoid of birds, cats, people, sunshine, and walks, if Veve was anything to go by.

"Veve!" If the sight of the mad Lab-rat barrelling toward them hadn't scared the birds off, my shouts would have. "Come back here *now*!"

Predictably, she ignored me, pounding down the slope, through the fringe of gum trees, and down the narrow stairs between giant granite boulders that led to the river.

"Stupid frogging brainless beast of a stupid frogging dog," I muttered as I followed. "If Mum gets home before we do and freaks out, I swear, I'll pluck your tail hairs out."

Empty threats, obviously, but Mum's freak-out wouldn't be. Her thoughts would go straight to the day Anna nearly died—and I wouldn't blame her.

I should have left a note. Urgh.

The stairs ended and I found myself on a track broad enough for two twisting along a creek the colour of bitter tea. Tussock grass clustered in spikes—where the eucalypts would let it—and hot summer sunlight glinted from the leaves. Somewhere to my right, downstream and in the opposite direction to the house, Veve barked. I exhaled like a whale coming up for air and set out after her.

Veve bounded out from the under-growth in front of me, a dolphin leaping through water, tongue flapping with every bound. "Stupid mutt," I told her under my breath.

She didn't care what I thought (of course), and saved a leap for the last minute so she could plant muddy feet on my hips as I tried to catch her collar.

I straightened, about to insult her some more, and realised that she'd gone stiff again, ears pricked and mouth tight, listening down the path.

My neck prickled. Someone was coming. A second later, I heard footsteps in the gravel, and a low, male voice, humming, or maybe singing softly.

My chest constricted, and just as suddenly my hands were slick. Chances were it was just a stranger out for a midday stroll, but my stomach wound knots about my memories and

I smelled the hot concrete and melting asphalt, old oil and stale urine of the Lilydale train station where the body had been hidden in a toilet stall, the body of the girl who'd looked like Anna.

I had to get off the path.

"Come on, Veve," I said, pulling her close, white-knuckled as I stepped into the undergrowth. The tea tree scrub protested, but I shoved my way through anyway, glancing over my shoulder as the humming grew louder.

I kept going until I couldn't hear footsteps any more, until the wind swallowed the hum that sounded too like the warning cry of a hive—danger, we're working here, come close and get stung. I didn't want to get stung; visions of a blood-streaked face refused to be blinked away.

Only Veve tugging brought me back to myself, and I realised firstly that I was holding the lead way too tight, cutting off Veve's air supply, secondly that the reason my cheeks were suddenly cold was because I'd been crying, and thirdly that I'd found the creek again, looping back parallel maybe fifty meters or so from the path.

Abruptly, I dropped Veve's lead and strode forward to kneel by the water. I dipped my hands in. A shiver slid through me at its chill, and I scooped it up to wash my face.

Flinging the excess water away, I gulped at the air, deep, calming breaths all the way down into my belly, and visualised a river washing away the blood from my thoughts, just like the police psych had taught me.

Once the space behind my eyes was calm and black, I drew in one last forceful breath, and opened my eyes. Perched on a rock by the creek, I hugged my knees to my chest as cool water lapped at my toes. Veve was a little upstream, just before the creek bent back toward the path, doggy paddling in circles in a deep spot where the water broadened to maybe ten meters across. In front of me it was broad but shallow, only ankle deep, its path torn to white foam by the rocks.

And—I gasped. In the middle of the stream, glittering in the sun like a piece of fallen sky, was the hugest butterfly I'd ever seen.

Which was pretty huge; besides the fact that I grew up visiting the Melbourne Zoo with its impressive butterfly house every Christmas since I could remember, Mum and Dad had taken us up to Brisbane for a family holiday two years ago, and we'd seen giant tropical butterflies bigger than my hand.

This one, bright blue with black edging like a Ulysses, was bigger than both my hands put together.

And then it turned around.

Okay. I'd grown up reading fairy tales as much as the next person, and although I'd had a horse-crazy stage instead of a fairy-crazy stage like Anna had, I'd seen all her paraphernalia.

Still, none of it prepared me for finding something that looked exactly like a fairy, standing smack in the middle of a creek in boring, back-water Nowra.

I'm pretty sure my eyes were only hanging in their sockets by a thread.

And then it talked.

Her face lit up like a cloud had just uncovered the sun as she spotted me. "Hi there!" she said, fluttering over.

I just stared, heart pounding against my ribcage as though it wanted to run away from the absurdity of it all. "No," I said. "I'm hallucinating."

The fairy frowned. "I don't think so."

I shook my head. "No. No, things like this do not happen. Things like this aren't *real*." I stood, backing up a step.

The fairy sighed. "I promise. I'm quite real."

"You would say that, wouldn't you," I said, eyeing her. "Veve!" I waved at the dog and hopped from one foot to the other, trying to lure her in with the promise of play. "We're going now!"

Veve, adorable beast that she was, landed a little upstream and shook vigorously before trotting toward me. I backed hurriedly away from the bank, dancing to keep Veve's attention.

"Wait!" the fairy cried, wings snapping out and propelling her a couple of feet into the air. "You're a Traveller! I need to talk to you!"

"Uh huh, sure," I said as I wound the lead around my hand and set off back into the bushes. This was punishment for leaving the house, obviously. The universe was out to get me, reminding me forcefully that once you started disregarding some rules, who knew what other rules you'd end up flouting.

The rules of physics, for example.

I glanced back once, right before the bushes hid the stream altogether. Blue flashed, high up, but I ducked to get a better view and it was only the sky. I scowled. Stupid fairy. Stupid universe. Served me right for leaving the house in the first place. Urgh. "Come on, Veve," I said, snapping the lead. "Even if the house is prison, at least it's *sane*."

I was stomping so furiously as I burst out onto the path that when a figure rose from a stoop only a couple of steps away, I squeaked in surprise.

I scowled. People rarely surprised me; usually I could tell without trying that someone was near. I really must have been off in my own little world.

I glowered at the boy who lived to make my school life a misery. "What are you doing here?" I snapped. "Isn't it bad enough that I have to deal with you on school days? Which, by the way, don't start until tomorrow. You're ruining my holidays."

Okay, so maybe that was a little harsh, but come on. It was *Scott*. I'd arrived in town with three weeks left in the school year, and he'd spent every day of them humiliating me in front of his mates, and I didn't care for a repeat this year.

Scott eyed me warily, which was a strange expression on him.

Usually he strode around like he knew without a doubt that he was too good for the world, and also—somewhere deeper, somewhere I'd only caught a glimpse of once or twice— that it had nothing left to throw at him that could hurt.

Occasionally, in my more generous moments, I wondered what had happened to make him look that way.

Mostly, however, I just wondered why he was such a moron.

"What are you doing here?" he asked, voice dripping with accusation and suspicion.

My hands fisted of their own accord, and beside me Veve's hackles rose as she chimed in with a low-pitched, rumbling growl. I flicked the free end of the lead at her nose. "Nothing," I said, in a rousing blaze of wit. "What are you doing?"

He scowled. "You shouldn't be here."

For one heart-stopping instant I thought he meant out here generally, walking around, as if he knew what had happened and why I'd hidden away all summer. Then I realised he was nodding into the undergrowth. I rolled my eyes. "I might be a city slicker," I bit off, "but I'm not stupid. I made enough noise to scare off a herd of elephants, let alone any snakes that might have been lying around." The thought chilled me, though; I *hadn't* been thinking about snakes when I'd hurried off the path. One badly-timed footstep and a brown snake bite later, and I could be a dead body too.

But Scott had moved on, stalking off down the path. He had nice shoulders, I'd give him that much. Pity he couldn't derive his personality from them, instead of whatever dead weight it was he kept inside his head for brains.

Beside me, Veve growled again, louder this time, more urgent. I snapped the lead at her and stared after Scott's retreating form, trying to think of something cutting.

It was only when Veve growled for the third time that I realised she wasn't even facing Scott. Instead, she was looking back into the bushes—and something dark was flickering in there, deep in the shadows of the trees.

My chest squeezed in on itself and adrenalin shot through my body. Veve's growling grew louder until it broke in a bark, something midway between slavering and terrified, and I realised my tongue was stuck to the roof of my mouth. Carefully I peeled it away, unable to tear my eyes from the shifting darkness in the bushes. There was no discernible form, just shadow, darker than it should have been this soon after midday, and a pervasive sense of dread clamping down on me like an on-coming storm.

Veve began backing away, hackles prickling, growl rising and falling like thunder. I glanced down at her, back to the shadows—and they were closer, much closer than they had been.

I turned and bolted.

Keep reading! Head to
www.amylaurens.com/books/sanctuary/where-shadows-rise/
to buy your copy now!

ABOUT THE AUTHOR

AMY LAURENS is an award-winning Australian author of fantasy fiction for all ages. She, like Beth, attended some creative writing classes at university, though she was probably not as good at writing then as Beth is.

In addition to moderately twisted little school stories, Amy has written the portal-fantasy *Sanctuary* series about Edge, a 13-year-old girl forced to move to a small country town because of witness protection (the first book is *Where Shadows Rise*); the humorous *Kaditeos* series, following newly-graduated Evil Overlord Mercury as she attempts to acquire a castle; the young adult *Storm Foxes* series about magic, love, and mental health; and a whole host of non-fiction.

See <u>www.amylaurens.com</u> for more.

INKLETS

Collect them all! Released on the 1ˢᵗ and 15ᵗʰ of each month.

Welcome to Dark Dale
LIANA BROOKS

When War Came to Town
A Powers Story
AMY LAURENS

Not Fantasy
AMY LAURENS

Courting the Winter Prince
LIANA BROOKS

At the Home of the Winter King
A Storm Foster Story
AMY LAURENS

With This Ring
AMY LAURENS

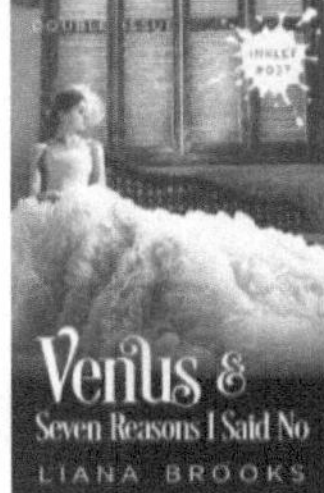

Venus &
Seven Reasons I Said No
LIANA BROOKS

OATH KEEPER
AMY LAURENS

FORGET
A Powers Story
AMY LAURENS

NOT QUITE
Cinderella
LIANA BROOKS

ONE BAD MAN
AMY LAURENS

DOUBLE ISSUE
The Claustrophobia
Of Loneliness &
Adam, Be A Star
AMY LAURENS

The Artist
as a Young Girl
LIANA BROOKS

CONFESSIONS
AMY LAURENS

But For Snow
A Railroos Story
AMY LAURENS

The Boy
Named NO
LIANA BROOKS

Anamata
AMY LAURENS

A Wolf FOR
Christmas
AMY LAURENS